DPT

1213

U.S. WARS

WORLD WAR I

A MyReportLinks.com Book

John Richard Conway, Esq.

MyReportLinks.com Books
an imprint of
Enslow Publishers, Inc.
Box 398, 40 Industrial Road
Berkeley Heights, NJ 07922
USA

MyReportLinks.com Books, an imprint of Enslow Publishers, Inc. MyReportLinks is a trademark of Enslow Publishers, Inc.

Copyright © 2003 by Enslow Publishers, Inc.

All rights reserved.

No part of this book may be reproduced by any means without the written permission of the publisher.

Library of Congress Cataloging-in-Publication Data

Conway, John R., 1969–
  World War I / John R. Conway.
    p. cm. — (U.S. wars)
  "A MyReportLinks.com Book."
  Summary: Discusses the major battles, military tactics, and famous figures of World War I. Includes Internet links to Web sites, source documents, and photographs related to the war.
  Includes bibliographical references and index.
  ISBN 0-7660-5142-0
  1. World War, 1914–1918—Juvenile literature. 2. World War, 1914–1918—United States—Juvenile literature. [1. World War, 1914–1918. 2. World War, 1914–1918—United States.] I. Title: World War 1. II. Title: World War One. III. Title. IV. Series.
  D522.7.C67 2003
  940.3—dc21
                    2002153590

Printed in the United States of America

10 9 8 7 6 5 4 3 2 1

To Our Readers:
Through the purchase of this book, you and your library gain access to the Report Links that specifically back up this book.
The Publisher will provide access to the Report Links that back up this book and will keep these Report Links up to date on **www.myreportlinks.com** for three years from the book's first publication date.
We have done our best to make sure all Internet addresses in this book were active and appropriate when we went to press. However, the author and the Publisher have no control over, and assume no liability for, the material available on those Internet sites or on other Web sites they may link to.
The usage of the MyReportLinks.com Books Web site is subject to the terms and conditions stated on the Usage Policy Statement on **www.myreportlinks.com**.
A password may be required to access the Report Links that back up this book. The password is found on the bottom of page 4 of this book.
Any comments or suggestions can be sent by e-mail to comments@myreportlinks.com or to the address on the back cover.

Photo Credits: AP/Wide World Photos, p. 18; British Broadcasting Corporation © 2001, p. 23; © Corel Corporation, p. 3; © Michael Duffy, 2000–03, p. 25; © New content 2001KCET, p. 16; © 7/8/99 W. Ira Boucher, p. 22; Enslow Publishers, Inc, pp. 14, 29, 44; Frank E. Schoonover, p. 1; Library of Congress, pp. 12, 38; MyReportLinks.com Books, p. 4; National Archives, pp. 21, 27, 34, 37, 39, 40, 43; Smithsonian Institution, p. 30.

Cover Photo: Frank E. Schoonover/USMC Museums Art Collection

Cover Description: *Marines at Belleau Wood*

Contents

	Report Links	**4**
	World War I Facts	**10**
1	**The Great War**	**11**
2	**The Storm Breaks**	**18**
3	**A New Style of War**	**25**
4	**Different Strategies**	**32**
5	**Help is on the Way**	**36**
6	**The End and the Aftermath**	**40**
	Chapter Notes	**46**
	Further Reading	**47**
	Index	**48**

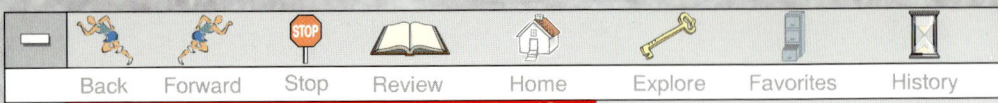

About MyReportLinks.com Books

MyReportLinks.com Books
Great Books, Great Links, Great for Research!

MyReportLinks.com Books present the information you need to learn about your report subject. In addition, they show you where to go on the Internet for more information. The pre-evaluated Report Links that back up this book are kept up to date on **www.myreportlinks.com**. With the purchase of a MyReportLinks.com Books title, you and your library gain access to the Report Links that specifically back up that book. The Report Links save hours of research time and link to dozens—even hundreds—of Web sites, source documents, and photos related to your report topic.

Please see "To Our Readers" on the Copyright page for important information about this book, the MyReportLinks.com Books Web site, and the Report Links that back up this book.

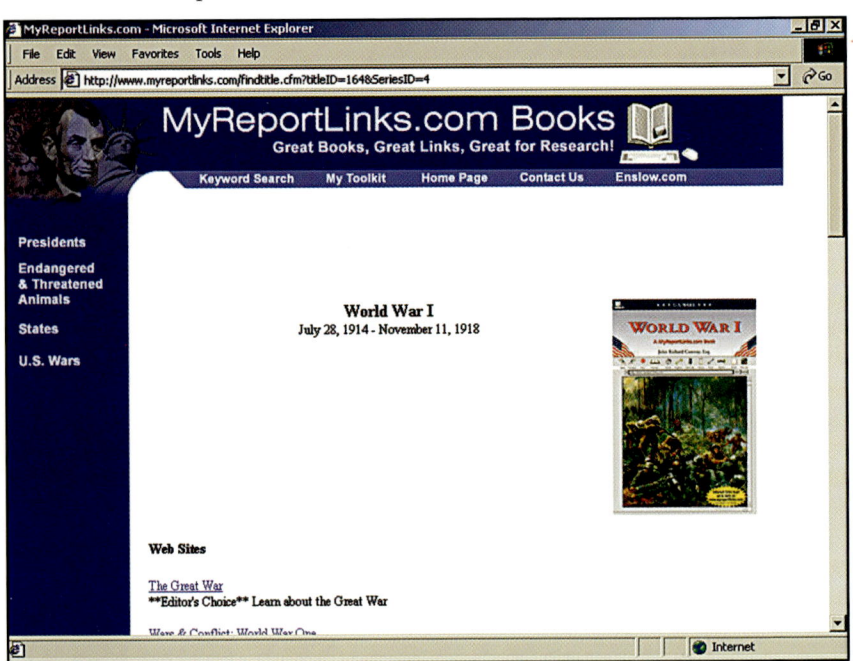

Access:

The Publisher will provide access to the Report Links that back up this book and will try to keep these Report Links up to date on our Web site for three years from the book's first publication date. Please enter **AWW4745** if asked for a password.

| Tools | Search | Notes | Discuss |  MyReportLinks.com Books | Go! |

Report Links

The Internet sites described below can be accessed at
http://www.myreportlinks.com

*Editor's choice

▶ The Great War
At this Web site you will learn about the Great War. You will also find time lines, maps, and interviews.

Link to this Internet site from http://www.myreportlinks.com

*Editor's choice

▶ Wars & Conflict: World War One
The Wars & Conflict Web site contains many articles related to World War I. Here you can read about the battles, the social impact of the war, debates, and much more.

Link to this Internet site from http://www.myreportlinks.com

*Editor's choice

▶ First World War.com
First World War is a comprehensive Web site where you will find a description of how World War I began, a time line, battles, photos, weapons of war, and interesting articles written about the war. You can also explore the war by month and year.

Link to this Internet site from http://www.myreportlinks.com

*Editor's choice

▶ The Great War: 80 years on
The Great War: 80 years on Web site contains letters written by soldiers, overviews of major battles, and many historical essays written about the war.

Link to this Internet site from http://www.myreportlinks.com

*Editor's choice

▶ Modern World History: The Treaty of Versailles
Here you will learn about the Treaty of Versailles, the key players in negotiating the treaty, and Germany and Italy's reaction to the treaty.

Link to this Internet site from http://www.myreportlinks.com

*Editor's choice

▶ The Aerodrome: Aces and Aircrafts of World War I
The Aerodrome Web site explores aces and aircrafts of World War I. This site contains a wealth of information about military ranks, aircraft statistics, medals and decorations, and much more.

Link to this Internet site from http://www.myreportlinks.com

Any comments? Contact us: **comments@myreportlinks.com**

Report Links

 The Internet sites described below can be accessed at
http://www.myreportlinks.com

▶American Forces Under General Pershing . . .
America's Story from America's Library, a Library of Congress Web site, tells the story of the United States first major offensive in World War I.

Link to this Internet site from http://www.myreportlinks.com

▶American Experience: Woodrow Wilson
This PBS Web site explores the life of Woodrow Wilson, president of the United States during World War I. Here you will find an interactive time line, a biography of Wilson, and other interesting facts about his life and administration.

Link to this Internet site from http://www.myreportlinks.com

▶The First World War: Sources for History
The First World War: Sources for History is a comprehensive Web site about the war. Here you will find maps, original documents, and a brief overview.

Link to this Internet site from http://www.myreportlinks.com

▶The Great War Series
The Great War Series Web site contains many articles about World War I. Here you can read summaries of the war on the Western and Eastern fronts and much more.

Link to this Internet site from http://www.myreportlinks.com

▶Jump Back in Time: Great War & Jazz Age (1914–1928)
America's Story from America's Library, a Library of Congress Web site, explores the United States home front during World War I. Here you will learn about the Jazz Age and read other interesting stories related to the Great War.

Link to this Internet site from http://www.myreportlinks.com

▶League of Nations
Infoplease.com provides a brief history of the League of Nations, the international organization set up after World War I. Here you will learn about its origins, successes, and failures.

Link to this Internet site from http://www.myreportlinks.com

Any comments? Contact us: comments@myreportlinks.com

 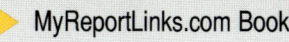

Tools Search Notes Discuss   Go!

Report Links

 The Internet sites described below can be accessed at
http://www.myreportlinks.com

▶ Legend, Memory and the Great War in the Air
This exhibit from the Smithsonian Institute explores aircraft combat in the Great War. Profiled here are the Fokker D. VII, SPAD XIII Smith IV, Sopwith Snipe, Voisin VIII LA.P, Albatros D. Va, and the Pfalz D. XII.

Link to this Internet site from http://www.myreportlinks.com

▶ Lost Liners: *Lusitania*
At this Web site you will find excerpts from the books *Lost Liners* and *Exploring the Lusitania.* They describe the events that took place on the day the *Lusitania* was sunk by a German U-boat.

Link to this Internet site from http://www.myreportlinks.com

▶ The Major Events of the Great War of 1914–1918
The Western Front Association Web site provides descriptions of many battles in World War I from 1914 through 1918.

Link to this Internet site from http://www.myreportlinks.com

▶ Modern World History: Russia in Revolution
At this Web site you will learn how the Russian Revolution began, the effects of World War I on Russia, and how the Bolshevik's were able to seize power.

Link to this Internet site from http://www.myreportlinks.com

▶ Nicholas II
During the Russian Revolution, Czar Nicholas II was overthrown. Factmonster.com provides a brief overview of his life and death.

Link to this Internet site from http://www.myreportlinks.com

▶ Searching for Gavrilo Princip
This article from *Smithsonian Magazine* discusses Gavrilo Princip, the teenage Serbian nationalist who shot Austrian Archduke Franz Ferdinand and propelled Europe into World War I.

Link to this Internet site from http://www.myreportlinks.com

Any comments? Contact us: **comments@myreportlinks.com**   7

Report Links

➤ The Internet sites described below can be accessed at
http://www.myreportlinks.com

▶ **Teaching With Documents Lesson Plan: The Zimmermann Telegram**
The National Archives and Records Administration provides background information on the Zimmerman Telegram. You can also view the coded and decoded letter.

Link to this Internet site from http://www.myreportlinks.com

▶ **Today In History: U.S. Enters World War I**
On April 6, 1917, the United States entered World War I. Here you will learn about that day and some events that led up to the United States' decision to enter the war.

Link to this Internet site from http://www.myreportlinks.com

▶ **Today In History: World War I**
This Web site explores the beginnings of World War I, Woodrow Wilson's "Fourteen Points" speech, and United States involvement in the war.

Link to this Internet site from http://www.myreportlinks.com

▶ **The Versailles Treaty: June 28, 1919**
The Avalon Project Web site holds the text of the Versailles Treaty. Here you can read all fifteen sections of the document that ended World War I.

Link to this Internet site from http://www.myreportlinks.com

▶ **Veterans Day**
America's Story from America's Library, a Library of Congress Web site, tells the story of Veterans Day, originally referred to as Armistice Day, which was celebrated at the end of World War I.

Link to this Internet site from http://www.myreportlinks.com

▶ **Visit Gallipoli**
The Visit Gallipoli Web site explores the events that took place on the Gallipoli Peninsula in Turkey during World War I. The heroic ANZAC troops are profiled, and there is a description of the building of the commemorative site.

Link to this Internet site from http://www.myreportlinks.com

Any comments? Contact us: comments@myreportlinks.com

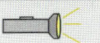
Tools   Search   Notes   Discuss   MyReportLinks.com Books   Go!

Report Links

 The Internet sites described below can be accessed at http://www.myreportlinks.com

▶ World War I
This Web site explores some key events in World War I, including the assassination of Archduke Franz Ferdinand, the gas attack in 1916, and the Battle at Gallipoli in 1915.

Link to this Internet site from http://www.myreportlinks.com

▶ wwiaviation.com: A Pictorial History of World War I
At this Web site you will find an overview of World War I. You can also learn about the men who operated aircrafts and other machines of war.

Link to this Internet site from http://www.myreportlinks.com

▶ World War I Document Archive
This Web site contains a vast amount of documents related to World War I. Here you will find official papers, treaties, a biographical dictionary, an image archive, and much more.

Link to this Internet site from http://www.myreportlinks.com

▶ World War I Ended With the Treaty of Versailles
America's Story from America's Library, a Library of Congress Web site, tells the story of the day World War I ended.

Link to this Internet site from http://www.myreportlinks.com

▶ World War I—1914–1918
This Web site provides a chronology of events leading up to World War I, the course of war, and the aftermath.

Link to this Internet site from http://www.myreportlinks.com

▶ World War I (1914–1918)
Infoplease.com provides a brief history of World War I. Here you will find an overview of major events that occurred from 1914 through 1918.

Link to this Internet site from http://www.myreportlinks.com

Any comments? Contact us: comments@myreportlinks.com

World War I Facts

▶ **Combatants**

Triple Entente/Allies: United States; France; United Kingdom; Russia; Serbia; Belgium; Greece; Italy; Japan; Montenegro; Portugal; Romania[1]

Triple Alliance/Central Powers: Austria-Hungary; Germany; Bulgaria; Turkey (Ottoman Empire)

1914—*June 28:* Archduke Franz Ferdinand and his wife, Sophie, are assassinated.

July 28: Austria-Hungary declares war on Serbia.

July 28 to August 6: Germany, Russia, France, and Great Britain declare war on each other.

July 29: Austria-Hungary invades Serbia but is defeated.

August: Germany invades France and Belgium.

August 17: Russia invades Germany.

October 29: Turkey joins the war.

1915—*May 7:* German U-Boat sinks the *Lusitania* passenger ship.

May 23: Italy declares war on the Central Powers.

November: Serbia is defeated.

1916—*August–December:* Romania enters the war on the side of the Allies.

1917—*January 31:* Germany again declares unrestricted U-boat warfare.

March 1: The Zimmerman Telegram is published.

April 6: United States declares war on Germany.

December 15: Russia's new Bolshevik government signs an armistice with Germany.

1918—*January 8:* Woodrow Wilson announces his Fourteen Points.

May 28: American troops win the Battle of Cantigny, their first major action.

May 30–June 17: The Americans win battles at Château-Thierry and recapture Belleau Wood.

September 29: Bulgaria signs an armistice.

October 30: Turkey signs an armistice.

November 3: Austria-Hungary agrees to an armistice.

November 11: Germany's armistice goes into effect.

November 23: Last of Germany's forces surrender in East Africa.

1919—*June 28:* The Treaty of Versailles is signed.

Chapter 1 ▶

The Great War

For the first time in nearly four years, the fields of Flanders were silent. Gone from the crisp fall air was the almost constant thunder of artillery fire. The local farms and bombed-out villages had become muddy and full of craters. It was 11:00 A.M. on November 11, 1918, and World War I, also known as the Great War and the War to End All Wars, had just ended.

Country	Killed/Died	Wounded	POW/MIA
ALLIES			
United States	116,516	204,002	0
United Kingdom	908,371	2,090,212	191,652
France	1,357,800	4,266,000	537,000
Russia	1,700,000	4,950,000	2,500,000
Serbia	45,000	133,148	152,958
Italy	650,000	947,000	600,000
Romania	335,706	120,000	80,000
CENTRAL POWERS			
Austria-Hungary	1,200,000	3,620,000	2,200,000
Germany	1,773,000	4,216,058	1,152,800
Bulgaria	87,500	152,390	27,029
Turkey (Ottoman Empire)	325,000	400,000	250,000

▲ A list of casualties for the major participants in World War I. It is estimated that more people died in World War I, than in all wars of the previous one hundred years.

Four years prior, men had gone off to war with parades, brass bands, and colorful uniforms expecting an easy victory. Virtually everyone thought that the war would be over quickly—that their sons, brothers, and husbands would be home by Christmas 1914. Nobody foresaw the agony that would bring down four massive empires and which saw the rise of a new industrial and military world power—the United States of America.

World War I was the first truly modern global conflict. It saw radical changes in military weaponry, tactics, and strategy. It saw the widening of the battlefield to include whole civilian populations distant from the actual fighting. World War I brought about the destruction of nineteenth-century imperialism and caused many major events of the twentieth century. Its aftermath can still be felt almost one hundred years later.

▶ The Storm Clouds Gather

In 1900, European countries were the most prosperous and powerful in the world. The largest of these colonial empires was Great Britain, also called the United

▲ At the end of World War I, much of Europe was devastated, including this no-man's-land in Flanders. No-man's-land is the area between enemy lines. This stretch of land often varied from less than thirty yards to more than one mile.

Kingdom. Britain ruled Australia, New Zealand, India, parts of China, large portions of southern and eastern Africa, Canada, many Caribbean islands, and even parts of South America.

▶ The British Empire

Britain had grown into the world's premiere manufacturing and financial power. Its navy was the most powerful force on earth. For the past two hundred years, the British waged an almost continuous war with France for colonial supremacy. However, in the nineteenth century, the French and British had essentially come to terms with each other. Meanwhile, a new colonial and naval rival, Germany, arose.

▶ Germany

Germany was a very young nation, only coming together when states of German-speaking peoples united after the Franco-Prussian War (1870–71). The new nation wanted to be a great world power and wanted overseas colonies. Germany started small colonies in Africa, the Pacific Islands, and China. To protect these colonies, Germany decided it needed a strong navy and began building new battleships and cruisers at a rate that alarmed both Britain and France. Furthermore, Germany's diplomatic policies had brought it into conflict with other powers on several occasions.

▶ France

The second-greatest colonial power in the world was France. Like Britain, France had a considerable overseas empire of colonies in Western Africa, Southeast Asia and the Pacific Islands, and parts of the Caribbean and South America. However, the French had been defeated by the

Germans in the Franco-Prussian War, and France was embarrassed because of it.[1] France was concerned that Germany was not finished with its aggressive political and military growth. As a result, it began seeking alliances with other countries.

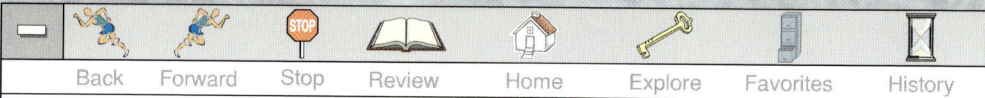

▲ A map of Europe before World War I.

Russia

Unlike France, Great Britain, or Germany, Russia had no colonies. Instead, Russia had created a massive connected land empire that covered much of eastern Europe and northern Asia. Russia, who had been militarily embarrassed several times in the nineteenth century, was eager to gain military glory and restore its reputation as a great power. Russia was also eager to gain territory at the hands of its old rival, Turkey, and be seen as the protector of all the Slavic peoples of eastern Europe.[2]

Austria-Hungary

The Austro-Hungarian Empire was a land empire that had emerged in the Middle Ages. It brought together many different ethnic groups into a single country under Emperor Franz Josef. Austria-Hungary was interested in expanding its presence into the Balkan Peninsula. This brought the nation into conflict with Russia, because Russia had an interest in the well-being of the Slavic people living in the Balkans. Austria-Hungary's primary concern, however, was keeping the various national and ethnic groups within the empire together. There were numerous terrorist groups that wanted to make parts of Austria-Hungary independent nations. It was these troubles that would eventually ignite World War I.

Turkey

Turkey, also known as the Ottoman Empire, was called "The Sick Man of Europe." Turkey was an ancient empire that at one time spanned three continents—Europe, Asia, and Africa. However, Turkey had been losing territory steadily in the nineteenth century. Early in the twentieth

century, Turkey had lost most of its European lands in a series of short, brutal wars.³ Turkey was also involved in a series of conflicts with the Russian Empire and wanted to regain some of its lost territory.

▶ The United States of America

The United States was just beginning to become a world power. It had recently defeated the Spanish Empire in the Spanish-American War. That war gave the United States possession of the island colonies such as Puerto Rico and the Philippines, and several other Pacific and Caribbean islands. Also, the United States had recently built the

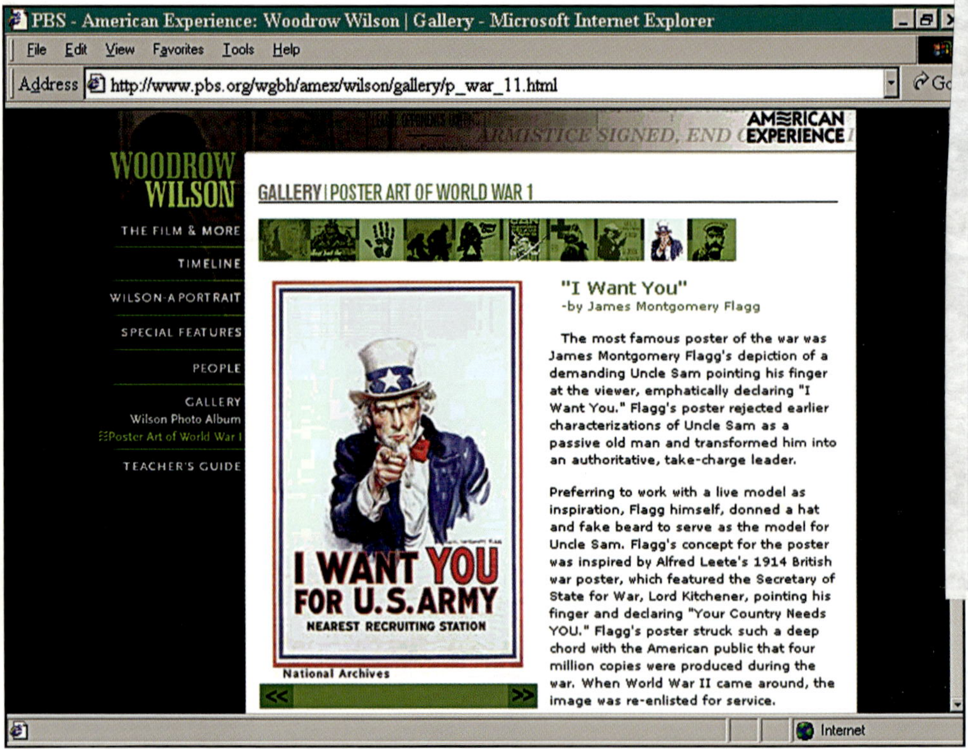

▲ In an effort to recruit troops, the American government distributed posters such as James Montgomery Flagg's Uncle Sam poster. This is one of the most famous images of the war.

Panama Canal and was involved alongside the European powers in several incidents in China. America was undergoing a massive industrial boom and was becoming a very wealthy country. However, at the outset of the twentieth century, America pursued a policy of isolationism. This meant the United States would stay out of world affairs unless they directly affected the country.

Secret Alliances

Due to these conflicting interests, these powers began to seek treaties and alliances to make sure that if a country was invaded, it had friends to help fight off the attacker. Germany, Austria-Hungary, and Italy formed the Triple Alliance. They were also known as the Central Powers. France, Russia, and Great Britain formed the Triple Entente. The Triple Entente became known as the Allies. Each of these powers also conducted secret alliances with other countries to ensure their participation or to make sure they would stay out of it if war ever came about. These secret alliances proved to be disastrous. They obliged larger countries and all their allies to become involved when smaller countries were attacked, thus dragging their allies into an unexpected and unwanted conflict.[4]

Chapter 2

The Storm Breaks

In June 1914, Archduke Franz Ferdinand, heir to the throne of Austria-Hungary, was traveling with his wife, Sophie. They were visiting the Austro-Hungarian province of Bosnia-Herzegovina near the province's capital, Sarajevo. Bosnia-Herzegovina was a province largely made up of Slavic Serbians, some of whom wanted Bosnia to become part of the neighboring kingdom of Serbia.

A group of Bosnian Serbians and Serbian army officers formed a terrorist group called "The Black Hand."

▲ Archduke Franz Ferdinand and his wife, Sophie, were shot and killed by nineteen-year-old Gavrilo Princip on June 28, 1914, while touring Sarajevo. This sparked the beginning of World War I.

This group of assassins wanted to end Austro-Hungarian rule in the area known as the Balkans.[1]

On the day of the visit, Gavrilo Princip, a member of the Black Hand, approached the archduke's car. Princip aimed a pistol at close range and fired twice at the archduke and his wife. Two shots hit, killing both of his targets.[2]

Austria-Hungary Reacts

There was no immediate proof of Serbian involvement in the assassination, but the government of Austria-Hungary held the Serbian government responsible. Austria-Hungary looked to its ally, Germany, for support in punishing Serbia. Germany's Kaiser Wilhelm told Austria-Hungary that they could count on Germany's support, even if this meant war with Russia. Austria-Hungary then presented Serbia with several demands meant to humiliate Serbia's government.[3]

The Serbians turned to their Russian allies for help. Russia agreed to support Serbia against the Austrians. They did recommend, however, that the Serbians comply with as many demands as possible. Serbia was willing to grant or discuss all the demands except one. The rejection of this single demand was seen by Austria-Hungary as cause for war.

The Austrians began shelling the Serbian capital city of Belgrade. By July 30, Russian Czar Nicholas II mobilized all of his troops for war. This move forced the Germans to order a complete mobilization of their forces.

It was obvious that many nations would become involved in the war because of the Russian alliance with France. The Germans knew that if Russia went to war, France was obligated by treaty to come to Russia's aid. This would cause Germany to fight a war on both sides of their country. Therefore, Germany made plans to defeat the French quickly, before the slow, but huge, Russian military could make its way to the battlefield. The German plan was to hold off the French along Germany's Western border, while the bulk of Germany's forces would march through Belgium. These troops would surround the main French armies, and seize Paris in a matter of weeks.[4] On August 1, Germany ordered a general mobilization and demanded that Belgium allow its armies free passage. Belgium refused because it was a neutral country. Germany began marching through Belgium anyway.

Great Britain, who was planning to remain neutral, became alarmed. It had treaties and historic ties in which Great Britain guaranteed Belgium's neutrality. On August 3, Britain sent Germany an ultimatum telling them to leave Belgium. That evening Germany declared war on France. Because Germany did not respond to Britain's ultimatum, a state of war began between Great Britain and Germany. At dawn the next day, Germany declared war on Belgium.

▶ The Early War

The declarations of war kept coming: Austria-Hungary formally declared war on Russia on August 5, Serbia declared war on Germany August 6, and France and Britain declared war on Austria-Hungary on August 10 and 12. Japan declared war against Germany on August 23 hoping to seize German possessions in China and the Pacific Ocean. Austria-Hungary responded by declaring war on Japan on August 25, and then declared war on Belgium on August 28.[5]

Italy, an ally of Austria-Hungary and Germany, remained neutral. Romania, who had a secret alliance with Germany, also stayed out of the war at that point in time.

The War in the West

The French commander, General Joseph Joffre, initiated the French war plan. The French made some headway into Germany at first, but then the German resistance stiffened and pushed the French army out of Germany.

Meanwhile, the Germans swept through Belgium and into northern France. They struck the small British Army that had come to assist the French at the village of Mons. The British, too, were forced to retreat.

The Germans faced problems too, because they were unable to get supplies to the soldiers quickly enough. The soldiers were becoming exhausted. Hearing that the Russian Army had already mobilized, German Commander Helmuth von Moltke ordered two corps of German soldiers east to face the Russians. This weakened the German advance against the French and British.

▲ The Germans wanted to make their way through Belgium to attack France. When the Belgians would not allow their free passage, Germany entered the country anyway in August 1914.

The French and British attacked the Germans and forced them back to the Aisne River. While waiting for the general staffs to make their next moves, the two sides started digging trenches.

In order to secure the flanks and possibly move around the enemy trenches, the Germans and the combined British and French armies continued to build trenches in what became known as the "Race to the Sea." From this point on, the war in the west took place in the defensive trenches that ran literally from the English Channel to Switzerland.

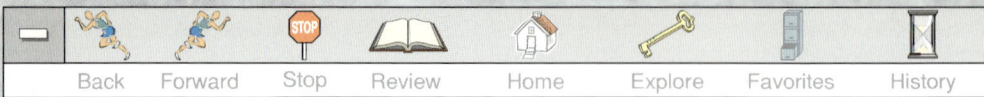

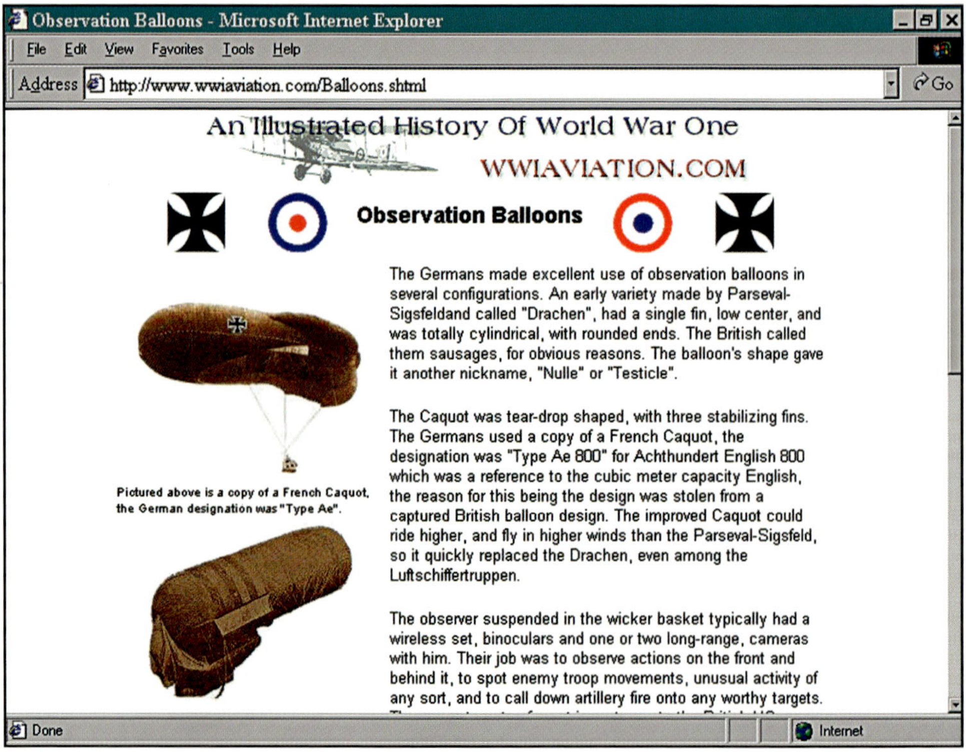

▲ The Germans put observation balloons to much use during World War I. These balloons were very hard to target as they were very well protected by long-range machine guns.

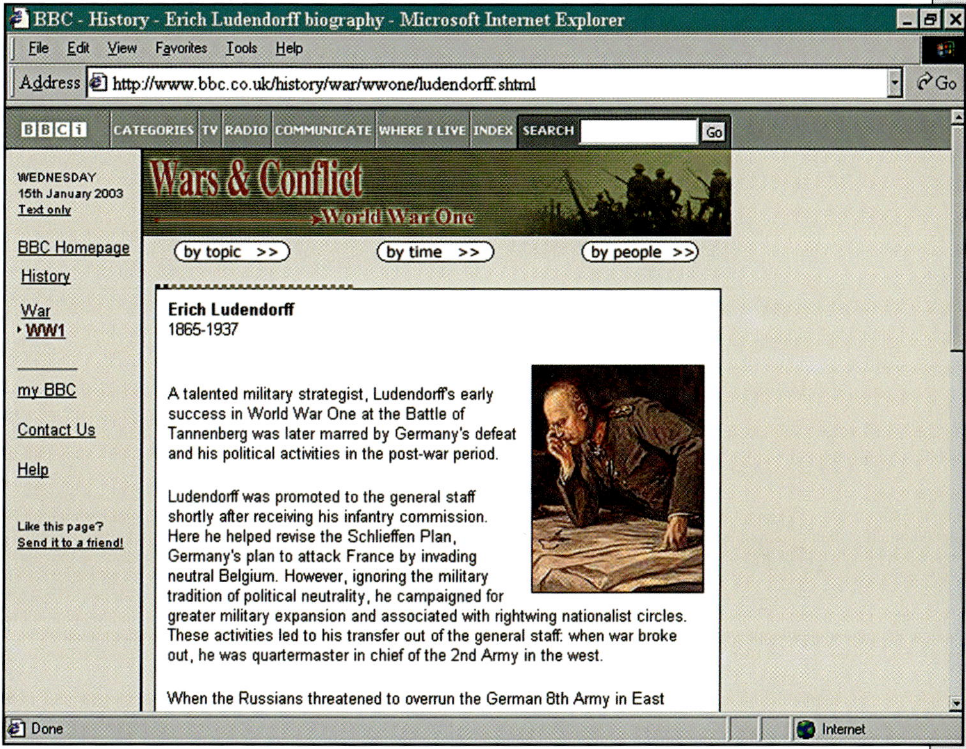

▲ General Erich Ludendorff was one of Germany's top military strategists. He approved Germany's unrestricted submarine warfare against Great Britain and refused to accept the terms of peace offered by the Allies.

▶ The War in the East

While the Germans were advancing against the French and British armies, the Russians moved into eastern Germany. The Russians had the world's largest army, with almost 6 million men and the capability of mobilizing 12 million. However, these men were poorly trained, badly equipped, and ineptly led.

On August 17, 1914, the Russians pushed into Germany, forcing the smaller German Army back in a series of indecisive conflicts. The Germans appointed two new leaders, Field Marshall Paul von Hindenburg, and his chief of staff General Erich Ludendorff, to take control of the eastern front. The Russian commander Alexander Samsonov confidently pushed his forces further into Germany for what he hoped would be a crushing blow against the Germans. On August 26, the German and Russian forces met at Tannenberg in Germany, where they fought for six days. The Battle of Tannenberg ended up being a terrible defeat for the Russian Army. A few weeks later, at the Battle of Masurian Lakes, the Russians were forced out of Germany.

Austria-Hungary's Campaigns

After bombarding the Serbian capital of Belgrade, the Austro-Hungarian Army invaded Serbia. The Austro-Hungarians expected an easy victory, but the Serbians counterattacked and forced the Austrians back into Austria-Hungary.

The Austrians also attempted to invade Russia. They defeated the Russian Army at the Battle of Krasnik (August 23–25) and the Battle of Zamosc-Komarow (August 26–September 1). However, the Russians managed to eventually beat back the Austrians.

On October 29, Turkey entered the war on the side of Germany and Austria-Hungary by bombarding the Russian Black Sea Fleet near the port cities of Sevastopol and Odesa on the Black Sea. The Turks hoped to regain territory lost to the Russians in previous wars. While Turkey presented no significant military threat to France or Great Britain, it did control the Dardanelles, a strait that was one of two ways to get badly-needed supplies to Russia. Without these supplies, it would be hard for the Russians to keep fighting.

Chapter 3 ▶

A New Style of War

After the first few months of the war, the countries found themselves fighting an entirely new style of warfare. In previous wars, large armies fought in lines. They depended on the firepower of their infantry, or foot soldiers, with cavalry providing the offensive punch and artillery support. Commanders on both sides thought that the new war

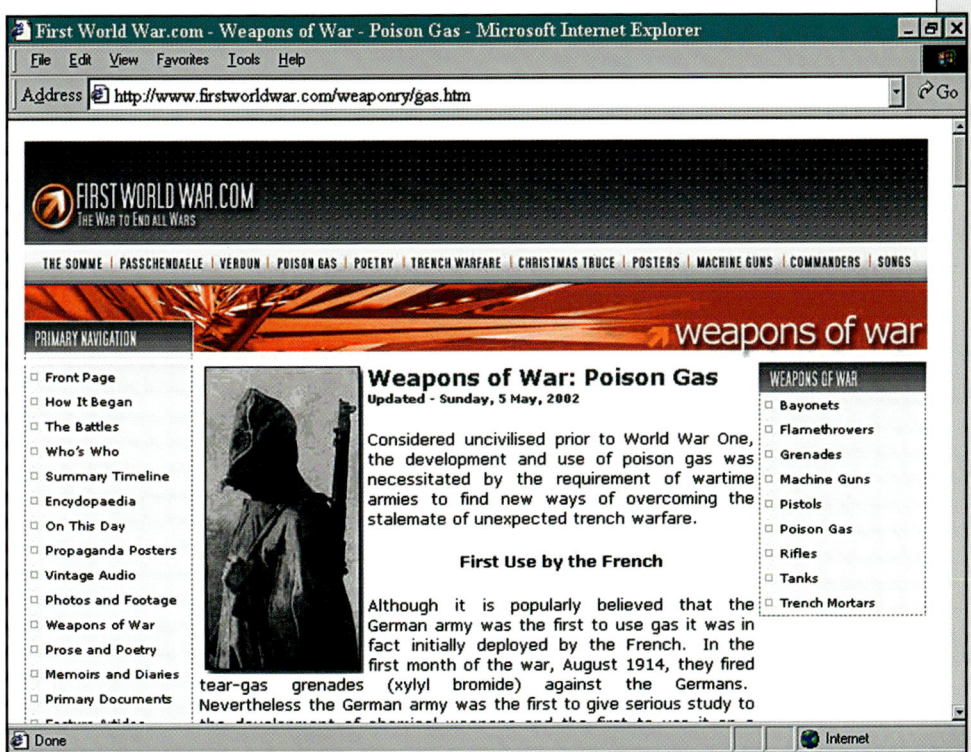

▲ The Germans were the first to use chemical warfare on a large scale. They first introduced poison gas on April 22, 1915, at the Second Battle of Ypres.

would be fought on similar principals. They were wrong, and it cost millions of men their lives.

▶ Changes in Warfare

The armies of World War I were the largest the world had seen. There were more men to move and supply than anyone had ever moved and supplied before. The supply systems that these countries used in the past were no longer helpful.

Secondly, due to changes in technology, the very nature of how wars would be fought had changed. The Germans discovered the use of the "Rolling Barrage." Before, the artillery had to stop before the infantry could advance on the enemy. This gave the armies time to regroup and face the enemy before an attack. Now the German artillery kept firing just in front of the advancing infantry, giving the enemy no time to recover and no warning before an attack. This tactic was extremely effective early in the war.[1]

The development of the machine gun fundamentally changed how wars were fought. Now two men had the ability to fire as many as six hundred bullets per minute at long ranges. This meant a few machine gunners could hide and simply shoot down the waves of attacking soldiers.

▶ Life in the Trenches

Once one side or the other dug into defensive positions and trenches, it made it virtually impossible for the other side to attack and defeat them. Both sides hurled hundreds of thousands of men at their enemy's trenches, suffering terrible casualties and not making any significant gains.[2] Life in these defensive works and trenches was miserable. Generally, trenches were laid out in a zigzag pattern. This prevented attackers from firing all the way down the

▲ The western front of the war was stalled by trench warfare until 1918. Troops would serve at the front line for a few days to a week. After that time they would rotate to the rear.

trench, and minimized the effects of artillery shell blasts. There were main trenches, usually two or three parallel trenches, so that if one fell to an enemy assault, there would be another line of defense. These were connected by small communications trenches. Ahead of the main trenches were smaller observation posts to watch the enemy trenches. Most trenches were five to six feet deep and had firing steps so that men could fire over the top.

All of the trenches were badly drained and usually muddy. They were often full of water, garbage, bodies, and human waste. They were home to fleas, lice, and rats. Bacterial infections and dysentery were common problems. Artillery shellings and the constant threat of enemy snipers made the trenches very dangerous. Food had to be brought up from the rear, and was often cold well before

it reached the lines. At night, heavier artillery blasts and raids from enemy trenches led to some of the most brutal fighting of the war.

The area between the trenches became a killing zone of barbed wire, land mines, mud, and bodies. This uneven land became known as no-man's-land. It had to be crossed every time the enemy was attacked. Troops would come out of the trenches on orders and attempt to make their way across no-man's-land in hopes of getting to the enemy trenches and driving the enemy out. This was done through hails of machine-gun, mortar, and artillery fire. It was called "Going over the top," because men had to pull themselves over the tops of the trenches.

▶ Deadlock on the Western Front

The use of trenches stalled movement on the western front. Both sides decided that to break the deadlock and win the war, they would need to develop new superweapons. The Germans introduced poison gas as a weapon on April 22, 1915, against French colonial troops near Ypres. It was a bigger success than even the Germans had imagined. Soon both sides were using poison gases of different types on one another.[3]

The British experimented with armored vehicles to provide protection and support of infantry when attacking enemy trenches. Initially called "landships," they were later known as tanks. By the end of the war, the British, French, and Germans had their own tank programs.[4]

▶ The Air War

Initially, both sides started using airplanes for scouting out enemy positions and aiming artillery. As the war progressed, pilots started firing pistols at each other as they flew their

▲ A map of the western front of the war.

missions. Soon both sides were mounting machine guns on their flimsy wooden airplanes. Groups of planes would hunt down each other. Battles between individual pilots were called "dogfights." These battles assured that one side or the other had control of the skies so they could watch the enemy from above. Every country quickly made heroes of the most successful pilots, called "aces," including America's

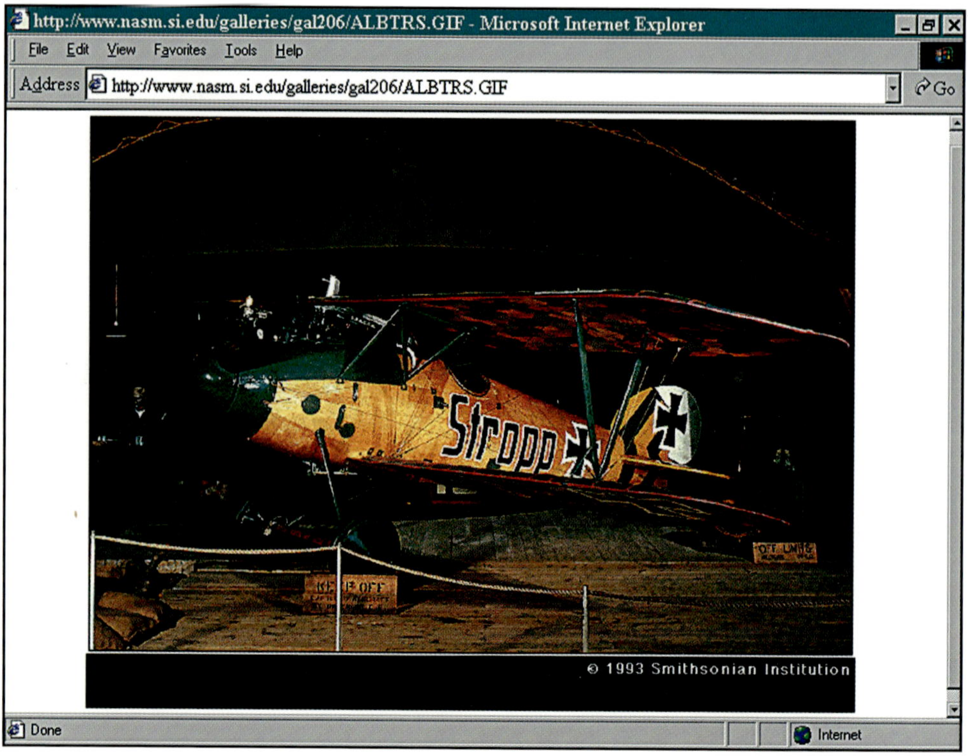

▲ *This Albatros D. Va was flown in the German offensive during March 1918. World War I was the first major war in which airplanes were used.*

Eddie Rickenbacker and Germany's Manfred von Richthofen, better known as "The Red Baron."

Germany also used zeppelins—massive airships that resemble blimps—to conduct bombing raids on civilian targets. The Germans opted to bomb several British cities, which caused little actual damage but had a great effect on the morale of both countries. The problem with zeppelins was that they were large, slow-moving airships filled with highly combustible hydrogen gas. The British used special bullets to explode them, making the zeppelins impractical for bombing purposes.[5]

The War at Sea

Initially, the British used their massive fleet to blockade Germany so that no supplies could get in or out of the country by ship. They hoped this would force Germany to surrender. Germany could not possibly blockade British ports with their surface navy (a fleet that sails on the water), so the Germans turned to a new weapon to cut off British supplies.

This new weapon was the submarine, or "U-boat" as the Germans called them. U-boats were dangerous because they moved underwater, then attacked suddenly and without warning. They proved very effective in sinking merchant ships in particular. The use of the U-boats was considered underhanded. If U-boats tried to capture or intercept a ship, people would know where it was. In order to stay undetected, U-boats would simply have to sink all of the ships in their path. The German government announced unrestricted submarine warfare in British territorial waters on February 4, 1915. This meant that they would sink any ship in British waters.

On May 7, a U-boat sank the British passenger liner *Lusitania*, killing 1,198 passengers, including 128 American citizens. President Woodrow Wilson had been determined not to involve the United States in the war. He decided to send the German government a strongly worded protest. After several other ships were sunk, followed by threats of American entry into the war, the German government temporarily suspended the unrestricted U-boat campaign.

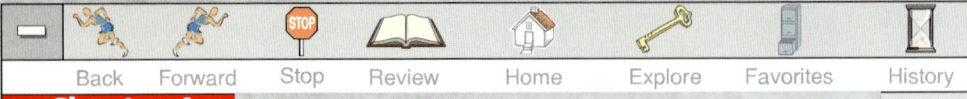

Chapter 4 ▶

Different Strategies

The British and French made several attempts to attack the Germans and push them back in 1915: Vimy Ridge, the Second Battle of Ypres, and Loos. All were failures in terms of lives wasted. Casualties for the year were estimated at 612,000 Germans, 279,000 British, and 1.29 million French troops killed or wounded with no significant gains on the enemy.[1] In hopes of breaking this deadlock, the British replaced their commanding general Sir John French with Sir Douglas Haig.

▶ Other Fronts

On May 23, 1915, Germany and Austria-Hungary's former ally, Italy, decided to join the war on the side of Great Britain and France. The Italian Army was large but poorly equipped. The Italians were defeated again and again by the Austro-Hungarian forces. Soon, the Italians and Austria-Hungary also ended up in immobile trench warfare.[2]

The Russians started off 1915 with another defeat at the hands of the Germans at the Second Battle of Masurian Lakes, also known as The Winter Battle. Two hundred thousand Russian men were killed or wounded. By June, the Germans had advanced more than three hundred miles into Russian territory, causing the Russians over a million casualties and capturing over a million more POWs.

On September 6, Bulgaria joined Austria-Hungary and Germany in the war. The Germans and Austrians launched an attack into Serbia while the Bulgarians attacked from the east. By the end of 1915, Serbia was out of the war.[3]

Disaster at Gallipoli

The Russians suffered from a lack of supplies from Britain and France. British planners, including Winston Churchill, were convinced that the straits of the Dardanelles, which were under Turkish control, could be the key to winning the war.[4] If these straits were taken by the British and French, then supplies could keep flowing into Russia. Occupation of the Dardanelles would require that the Germans remove soldiers and supplies from the western front. The British hoped this would weaken the Germans.

The British Navy began landing troops onto the beaches at Gallipoli near the mouth of the strait. Called the Australian and New Zealand Army Corps (ANZAC), these troops largely came from the South Pacific. As elsewhere in Europe, the Gallipoli invasion bogged down into trench warfare. The Allies became discouraged, and by December, the British had evacuated.

Attrition and Exhaustion

At the end of 1915, the Germans determined that they needed to defeat France and Russia in order to get the British to end the war. Rather than attempt to break a hole in the massive defensive works through an assault, they planned to weaken the French Army with casualties so that they would not have the strength to resist.[5]

Germans would accomplish this at the historic fortress of Verdun. The bombardment began on February 21, 1916. With the fall of one of the outer forts, General Henri Philippe Petain took over the French forces defending Verdun. A determined man he declared, "Ils ne passeront pas"—"They shall not pass." This became the French rallying cry for the rest of the war.[6]

▲ *Australian troops, part of the ANZAC, charge a Turkish trench on Gallipoli Peninsula. They landed in the area on April 25, 1915, and were not evacuated until December 1915 and January 1916.*

General Petain made supplying the fortress at Verdun his number-one priority, which played into German plans. What the Germans had not planned on was the unexpectedly stiff French resistance. By the end of year, French casualties had reached 400,000, but the German casualties of 350,000 made the assault more damaging than it was worth.

▶ The Brusilov Offensive

The Russians managed to gain a lot of ground in 1916. General Aleksei Brusilov, commander of the Russian armies facing Austria-Hungary, made a push on the Austrian armies and routed them. The Germans rushed help to their Austrian allies and slowed the Russian advance. Brusilov's soldiers began running out of supplies as the offensive came to a halt. This cost Russia its last best chance to win the war.[7]

The success of the attack convinced Romania that the Russians might have a chance to win the war. Romania ignored its treaty with Germany and joined the war on the side of the Allies. However, the Romanians were quickly defeated.

The Middle East and Mesopotamia

Turkey was busy with campaigns against the British and Arabs in the Middle East and Mesopotamia. The Turkish were slowly forced to give ground in the desert. They had the help of T. E. Lawrence, a British officer from Wales, who helped the Arabs fight the Turks. Lawrence is commonly referred to as "Lawrence of Arabia."

Jutland

The largest battle between battle fleets during the war was fought sixty miles off the coast of Jutland, Denmark. The action that followed cost the British heavily: 3 battle cruisers, 3 cruisers, and 8 destroyers, and 6,097 officers and men. The Germans lost one battleship, a battle cruiser, 4 light cruisers, 5 destroyers, and 2,551 officers and men.[8] The German High Seas Fleet decided to return to Germany.

Jutland was critical, because the British Navy retained control of the sea. This allowed them to supply Great Britain and its ally's war effort, and maintain the choking blockade on Germany. If the Germans had managed to defeat the British, the British war effort would probably have been doomed. Great Britain depended on supplies sent by ship from the colonies and from the United States. Jutland was also critical because it forced Germany to abandon surface threats to shipping again and reinstitute unrestricted submarine warfare against Great Britain. This move ultimately brought the United States into the war on the side of Britain and France.

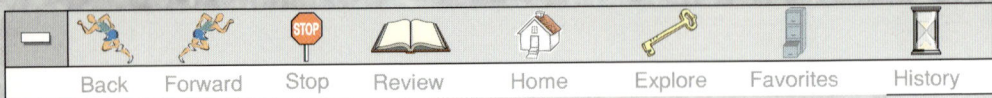

Chapter 5 ▶

Help is on the Way

On January 31, German government announced that it would resume unrestricted submarine warfare. Four days later, a U-boat sank the USS *Housatonic*. The United States protested vigorously, and President Woodrow Wilson authorized that American merchant ships be armed to be used to defend themselves only if attacked. This policy was referred to as *armed neutrality*.

▶ American Entry Into the War

The British had intercepted a telegram from German Foreign Minister Alfred Zimmerman to the Mexican government. The telegram proposed an alliance that would bring Mexico into the war on the German side. In exchange, Mexico would get back much of the territory it lost during the Mexican-American War once the United States was defeated. Wilson was outraged when he read it and had the telegram published in newspapers on March 1 to see what the public's opinion would be.

The "Zimmerman Telegram," along with existing tensions between the United States and Germany, made war inevitable. On April 6, 1917, the United States declared war on Germany. In Wilson's words, "The world must be made safe for democracy." Still, the president had misgivings. During the applause after his speech declaring war, Wilson said to his personal secretary, "Think what they are applauding. My message today was a message of death to our young men."[1]

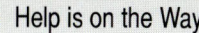

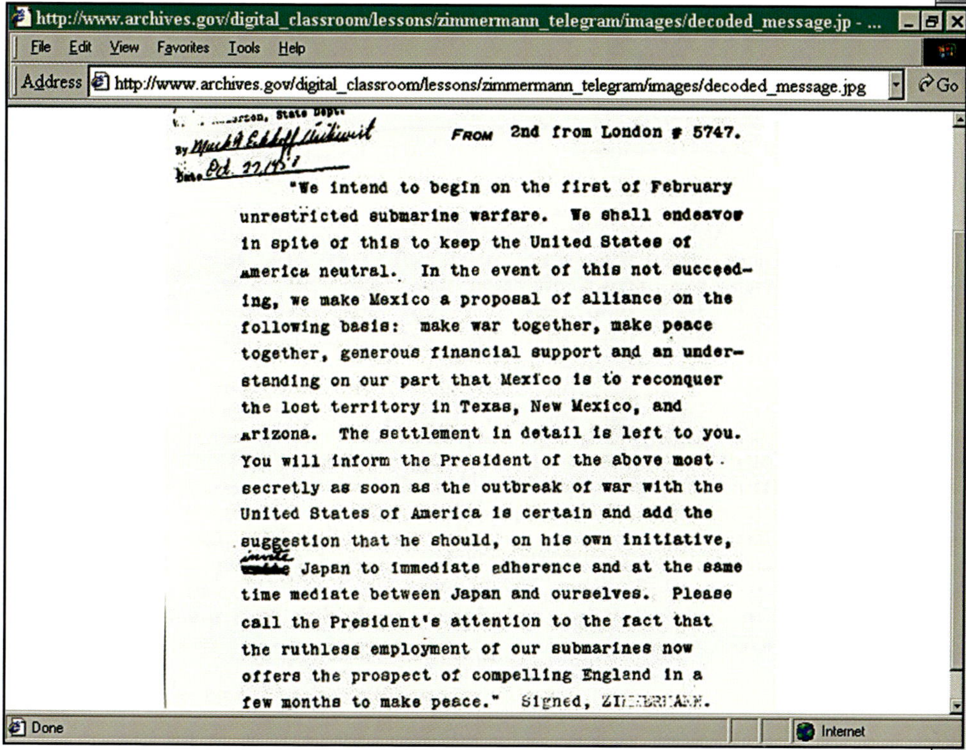

> "We intend to begin on the first of February unrestricted submarine warfare. We shall endeavor in spite of this to keep the United States of America neutral. In the event of this not succeeding, we make Mexico a proposal of alliance on the following basis: make war together, make peace together, generous financial support and an understanding on our part that Mexico is to reconquer the lost territory in Texas, New Mexico, and Arizona. The settlement in detail is left to you. You will inform the President of the above most secretly as soon as the outbreak of war with the United States of America is certain and add the suggestion that he should, on his own initiative, invite Japan to immediate adherence and at the same time mediate between Japan and ourselves. Please call the President's attention to the fact that the ruthless employment of our submarines now offers the prospect of compelling England in a few months to make peace." Signed, ZIMMERMANN.

▲ German Foreign Minister Arthur Zimmerman sent a telegram to Mexico. He offered German financial assistance and the return of Texas, New Mexico, and Arizona, in exchange for Mexico's support in the war.

▶ The Hindenburg Line

The American entry into the war came at a critical time for the Allies. The Germans had defeated every Allied attempt to break the deadlock in the west and had the Russians more or less defeated in the east. The Germans created a defensive position known to the Allies as the Hindenburg Line. This position would be very difficult for the French and British to break through.

▶ French Army Rebellion

France's next offensive cost 120,000 French casualties in five days. The French soldiers had had enough. On April

President Woodrow Wilson announced a declaration of war against Germany on April 6, 1917. This was less than three months after U.S.-German diplomatic relations had officially been broken.

29, veteran French regiments began to rebel. The soldiers pledged to defend the trenches but refused to attack. By June, only two reliable French divisions lay between the Germans and Paris. Luckily for the Allies, the Germans did not hear about the mutiny. French commander Petain managed to quiet the soldier's concerns with improved food and medical care. He also promised that there would only be local attacks rather than major offensives. Petain was hoping to hold out until the United States Army arrived with fresh troops.

Disgusted with the French Army, British General Haig decided that the British would have to bear the brunt of offensive action on the Western Front. On July 31, Haig began the Third Ypres offensive, better known as the Battle of Passchendaele. The British managed to take the town and advance roughly five miles at a cost of three hundred thousand casualties.[2]

▶ "Laffayette, We Are Here"

On June 14, American General John "Black Jack" Pershing landed with a small force of American soldiers. Upon landing, Colonel Charles Stanton said, "Lafayette, we are here." The United States was now returning a favor to the French for helping win American independence in the American Revolution.[3] The small staff was in France to organize the American effort of sending troops in bulk to Europe. This was the first time that United States had ever sent a major army overseas. However, the troops would not arrive until 1918.

Other Fronts

In March, food riots broke out in the Russian capital of St. Petersburg. These riots escalated to the point where Czar Nicholas II was forced to give up the throne. The Duma (the Russian Parliament) appointed a provisional government. The German government paid and transported an exiled Russian leader of the communist Bolshevik party, Vladimir Ilyich Lenin, from Switzerland to Russia.[4]

The Bolsheviks, led by Lenin, revolted and overthrew the provisional government. One of the first acts of the Bolshevik government was to end Russia's participation in the war.[5] A truce with Germany was signed on December 2 and formalized by the Treaty of Brest-Litovsk. Hundreds of thousands of German troops could now join the fight on the western front.

General John "Black Jack" Pershing served as commander-in-chief of the American Expeditionary Force in Europe. In 1921, he was appointed U.S. Army Chief of Staff.

Chapter 6

The End and the Aftermath

As the United States Army began building its military and preparing to send it to Europe, President Wilson attempted to end the war by peaceful means. On January 8, 1918, he announced his Fourteen Points. The most well-known point was the creation of an international League of Nations to assure political independence and territorial integrity. These points were disputed more by Wilson's allies, the British and the French, than the German enemy.[1]

German commander General Ludendorff planned for a final knockout blow against the British and the French.

▲ *From left to right: General von Hindenburg, Kaiser Wilhelm, and General Ludendorff study plans in January 1917.*

On March 21, he launched his first of five offensives. He attacked the British at the Somme and forced a forty-mile breakthrough, the most movement on the Western Front since 1914. Ludendorff then launched a second offensive at Lys. With the British army on the verge of collapse, General Haig gave the General Order of the Day, April 12, 1918, the famous "backs to the wall" order. Haig ordered the British army to hold their ground to the death since there were no reinforcements. Despite the pounding the British forces had taken, they managed to hold on and even push the Germans back.

Ludendorff turned his attention toward the French forces and launched an offensive against the Aisne River. The attack was so successful that the Germans pushed to within fifty miles of Paris. The inexperienced American troops were rushed to Cantigny where they managed to stop the German attack.

The American Army also fought engagements at Château-Thierry, and United States Marines captured Belleau Wood from the Germans.

Ludendorff ordered yet another offensive at Noyon-Montdidier in France. This advance was stopped by French and American forces. Finally, Ludendorff ordered a general advance against both the British and French at the same time. This offensive was also beaten back as the German Army exhausted itself. Furthermore, the Germans were running out of food and equipment because of the British blockade.

▶ The End of Austria-Hungary, Bulgaria, and Turkey

General Ludendorff withdrew German forces from the Italian front, leaving Austria-Hungary to face the Italians alone. With some British and American assistance, the

Austrian army collapsed under pressure. On November 4, 1918, the Austro-Hungarian Empire signed a truce.

Bulgaria had already signed a truce on September 29. Turkey was also knocked out of the war by British pressure in Mesopotamia and the Middle East. Turkey had agreed to a truce on October 30, 1918.

Germany Stands Alone

The Allies began another offensive on the western front against Germany. Known as the Amiens Offensive, the plan managed to push the Germans back to the Hindenburg Line. In October, the Americans began their campaign in Argonne Forest with the intention of cutting off German supply lines. At the end of October, sailors from the German High Seas Fleet stuck in Kiel Harbor rebelled. Without the German kaiser's permission, the German chancellor announced that Kaiser Wilhelm gave up his power on November 9. The next day, the Kaiser fled across the border into the Netherlands. A German republic was immediately declared and the German negotiations for peace were sped up. In a train coach at Compiegne, the German peace delegation signed truce at 5:00 A.M. on November 11, 1918. World War I was officially over at 11:00 A.M that day.

The Aftermath

On January 18, 1919, the leaders of France, Britain, Italy, and the United States met at the Palace of Versailles near Paris. They were there to work out the exact details of the peace. Germany and Austria-Hungary did not have representatives at this meeting, and the terms of the peace were dictated, not negotiated. The defeated nations had to give up huge amounts of land. They also had to pay very

▲ The Treaty of Versailles ended World War I in January 1919. In Paris, France, President Woodrow Wilson sits with the American Peace Commission to negotiate the terms of the treaty.

steep reparations (payments for the damages done to the winning countries). Germany was forced to admit that German aggression had actually started the war. The German Army was limited to a small force of 100,000 men. Germany's production of tanks, planes, submarines, and many other war materials was outlawed. Germany lost all of its overseas colonies and Austria-Hungary was dismantled, creating new countries of Austria, Hungary, Czechoslovakia, and Yugoslavia. A new country, Poland, was carved out of Germany and Russia. The treaty also set up the League of Nations, as Wilson had desired in his Fourteen Points.[2]

    The Treaty of Versailles was intended to end all wars. It failed miserably. The steep demands on Germany caused great resentment among Germans. The reparations crippled the German economy, and the loss of territory and military strength humiliated the people. These humiliations made the new German democracy appear to be

▲ A map of Europe after World War I.

weak, and set the stage for the rise of Adolf Hitler, his Nazi Party, and World War II.

The League of Nations was dealt a significant blow when the United States Senate decided not to ratify the Treaty of Versailles or join its League of Nations. This failure was a devastating blow to President Wilson, one that broke his spirit and wrecked his health. Without American support, the League of Nations was doomed. The United Nations, later established after World War II, was based on Wilson's idea of the League of Nations.

The impact of the Treaty of Versailles was still felt at the start of the twenty-first century. The treaty freed several different peoples from Austria-Hungary, but then pushed them back together as a single country called Yugoslavia. Conflict among the different nationalities of people living in Yugoslavia caused its collapse in the early 1990s. It sparked brutal and ongoing local warfare.

There were other consequences of World War I. The weapons first used in World War I set the style of warfare for the rest of the century. Airplanes, tanks, and submarines are all critical weapons in the arsenal of all major powers and formed the backbone of militaries in future conflicts.

Perhaps the most important effect of World War I may have been the experience gained by the United States. The war transformed the country into one of the primary superpowers of the world. The United States briefly tried to avoid getting involved in world conflicts after the war, but soon the country had developed a more active world outlook. World War I continued pushing the United States into becoming a leader in the world community.

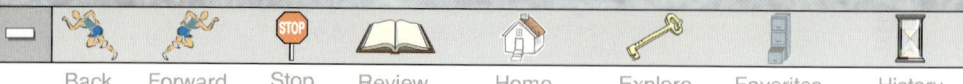

Chapter Notes

World War I Facts
1. Other nations joined the Allies, but these were the only ones to sustain casualties.

Chapter 1. The Great War
1. Philip Haythornthwaite, *The World War One Source Book* (London: Arms and Armor, 1999), pp. 11–12.
2. James L. Stokesbury, *A Short History of World War I* (New York: William Morrow and Company, 1981), pp. 20–21.
3. Ibid., pp. 19–20.
4. S. L. A. Marshall, *The American Heritage History of World War I* (Hong Kong: Bonanza Books, 1982), pp. 22–24.

Chapter 2. The Storm Breaks
1. James L. Stokesbury, *A Short History of World War I* (New York: William Morrow and Company, 1981), p. 23.
2. Ibid., pp. 23–24.
3. Hew Strachan, *The Oxford Illustrated History of the First World War* (New York: Oxford University Press, 2000), p. 19.
4. Ibid., p. 23.
5. John Terraine, *The Great War* (Ware, Hertfordshire: Wordsworth Military Library, 1999), p. 142.

Chapter 3. A New Style of War
1. Philip Haythornthwaite, *The World War One Source Book* (London: Arms and Armor, 1999), pp. 77–79.
2. Ibid., p. 70.
3. Ibid., pp. 90–92.
4. Ibid., pp. 95–99.
5. Ibid., pp. 117–118.

Chapter 4. Different Strategies
1. James L. Stokesbury, *A Short History of World War I* (New York: William Morrow and Company, 1981), p. 101.
2. Ibid., pp. 108–109.
3. Hew Strachan, *The Oxford Illustrated History of the First World War* (New York: Oxford University Press, 2000), pp. 69–70.
4. John Terraine, *The Great War* (Ware, Hertfordshire: Wordsworth Military Library, 1999), p. 205.
5. Ibid.
6. Ibid., p. 194.
7. Stokesbury, pp. 166–167.
8. Terraine, p. 237.

Chapter 5. Help is on the Way
1. S. L. A. Marshall, *The American Heritage History of World War I* (Hong Kong: Bonanza Books, 1982), p. 205.
2. Ibid., p. 274.
3. Ibid., p. 212.
4. James L. Stokesbury, *A Short History of World War I* (New York: William Morrow and Company, 1981), p. 210.
5. Ibid., p. 213.

Chapter 6. The End and the Aftermath
1. James L. Stokesbury, *A Short History of World War I* (New York: William Morrow and Company, 1981), pp. 301–302.
2. Hew Strachan, *The Oxford Illustrated History of the First World War* (New York: Oxford University Press, 2000), pp. 295–299.

Further Reading

Adams, Simon. *Eyewitness: World War I.* New York: Dorling Kindersley Publishing, 2001.

Allan, Tony. *The Causes of World War I.* Chicago: Heinemann Library, 2002.

Clare, John D., ed. *The First World War.* New York: Harcourt Children's Books, 1995.

Coetzee, Frans, et. al. *World War I: A History in Documents.* New York: Oxford University Press, 2002.

Dowswell, Paul. *Weapons and Technology of World War I.* Chicago: Heinemann Library, 2002.

George, Linda S. *Letters From the Homefront: World War I.* Tarrytown, N.Y.: Marshall Cavendish, 2001.

Gilbert, Adrian. *Going to War in World War I.* Danbury, Conn.: Franklin Watts, 2001.

Graves, Robert. *Good-Bye To All That: An Autobiography.* New York: Doubleday Publishing Group, 1998.

Hay, Jeff, ed. *The Treaty of Versailles.* Farmington Hills, Mich.: Greenhaven Press, 2002.

Kent, Zachary. *World War I: "The War to End Wars."* Hillside, N.J.: Enslow Publishers, Inc., 1994.

Ross, Stewart. *Assassination in Sarajevo: The Trigger for World War I.* Chicago: Heinemann Library, 2001.

———. *Causes and Consequences of World War I.* Austin, Tex.: Raintree-Steck Vaughn, 1998.

Strachan, Hew. *The Oxford Illustrated History of the First World War.* New York: Oxford University Press, 2000.

Tuchman, Barbara. *The Guns of August.* New York: Ballantine Books, 1994.

Index

A
aftermath, 12, 42–45
alliances, 17, 20, 33, 35, 37
ANZAC, 33
armed neutrality, 36
Austria-Hungary, 15, 18–20, 24, 32, 41–43

B
battles
　Argonne Forest, 42
　Belleau Wood, 41
　Cantigny, 41
　Château-Thierry, 41
　Flanders, 11
　Gallipoli, 33
　Jutland, 35
　Krosnik, 24
　Loos, 32
　Masurian Lakes, 24
　Masurian Lakes II, 32
　Tannenburg, 24
　Verdun, 33–34
　Ypres I, 28
　Ypres II, 32
　Ypres III (Passchendaele), 38
　Zamosc-Komarow, 24
Belgium, 20–21
Brusilov Offensive, 34–35
Bulgaria, 32, 42

C
casualties, 11, 32, 34, 37
Czar Nicholas II, 19, 39

F
Ferdinand, Franz, 18–19
Fourteen Points, 40, 43
France, 13–14, 20–21, 24, 32–33, 35, 39, 42

G
Germany, 13–14, 19–21, 23–24, 30–32, 34–35, 39, 42–43
Great Britain, 12–14, 20, 24, 32–33, 35, 42

H
Haig, Douglas, 32, 38, 41
Hindenburg Line, 37, 42
Hitler, Adolf, 44

I
Isolationism, 17

J
Italy, 20, 32

J
Joffre, Joseph, 21

K
Kaiser Wilhelm II, 19, 40, 42

L
Lawrence of Arabia, 35
League of Nations, 40, 43–45
Lenin, Vladimir Ilyich, 39
Ludendorff, Erich, 23–24, 40–44
Lusitania, 31

N
no-man's-land, 28

P
Pershing, John, 38–39
Petain, Henri Philippe, 33–34, 38
Poland, 43
Princip, Gavrilo, 19

R
Race to the Sea, 22
Red Baron, 30
Rickenbacker, Eddie, 30
Russia, 14–15, 19–20, 24, 33–34, 39, 43

S
Serbia, 18–19, 32
Stanton, Charles, 38–39

T
The Black Hand, 18
Treaty of Brest-Litovsk, 39
Treaty of Versailles, 43–45
trench warfare, 26–28
Triple Alliance (Central Powers), 17
Triple Entente (Allies), 17
Turkey, 15, 24, 35, 42

U
U-boats, 31, 36
United Nations, 45
United States, 12, 16–17, 35–36, 39, 45

V
von Hindenburg, Paul, 23–24, 40

W
warfare, 22, 25–31, 32–33, 45
Wilson, Woodrow, 36, 38, 40, 43–45

Z
Zimmerman Telegram, 36

5. Communication

Teachers can not read your mind or your child's mind. Healthy communication provides information not criticism. If your child is a visual learner, but the homework did not provide a visual sample, the teacher needs to know your child struggled. A teacher would never intentionally set up to dilute your child's learning. Re-teaching sheets can be sent home. Upfront agreed upon parent sign-off can be discussed when effort has been made, but homework is still too challenging. There are many options and resources available to the teacher, but if you do not communicate, she will not know.

6. Anxiety

Most children are people pleasers and having competing agendas with adults involved in their lives can only produce stress. Stress does not foster learning. When a person is stressed, they lose their train of thoughts and ability to process information effectively. Work hard for all adults to stay focused on the same page.

7. Love of learning

If your child desires to please you or your teacher too much, they will place an unhealthy pressure on himself to perform. That choice creates anxiety which affects